Developing Reader titles are ideal f
using their phonics knowledge and
with only a little help. Frequently repeated words …
fluency and confidence.

Special features:

Short, simple sentences

Everyone was at the dentist's.

"I am Mrs Yak," said the dentist.
"Welcome!"

"I like your big chair," said
Zara Penguin.

10

"You can get in it, if you like!"
said Mrs Yak.

So Zara did.

11

Frequent
repetition of
main story words
and phrases

Careful match
between story
and pictures

Large, clear
type

Nisha saw Mrs Yak's tools.

"This tool helps clean your
teeth and keep them healthy,
Nisha," said Mrs Yak. "It is very
gentle – look!"

Mrs Yak cleaned Nisha's teeth
with the gentle tool.

20

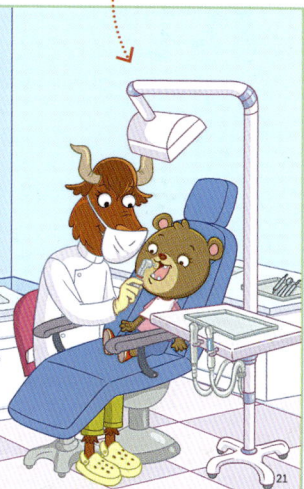

21

Educational Consultant: James Clements
Book Banding Consultant: Kate Ruttle
Subject Consultant: Nzinga Aidoo-Bell

LADYBIRD BOOKS

UK | USA | Canada | Ireland | Australia
India | New Zealand | South Africa

Ladybird Books is part of the Penguin Random House group of companies
whose addresses can be found at global.penguinrandomhouse.com.

www.penguin.co.uk   www.puffin.co.uk   www.ladybird.co.uk

Penguin
Random House
UK

First published 2025
001

Story by Ellen Philpott
Written by Catherine Baker
Text copyright © Ladybird Books Ltd, 2025
Illustrations by Jorge Santillan
Illustrations copyright © Ladybird Books Ltd, 2025
With thanks to Child Autism UK and Pace

The moral right of the illustrator has been asserted

Printed in Dubai

The authorized representative in the EEA is Penguin Random House Ireland,
Morrison Chambers, 32 Nassau Street, Dublin D02 YH68

A CIP catalogue record for this book is available from the British Library

ISBN: 978-0-241-67417-8

All correspondence to:
Ladybird Books
Penguin Random House Children's
One Embassy Gardens, 8 Viaduct Gardens, London SW11 7BW

Written by Catherine Baker
Illustrated by Jorge Santillan

"Look at this book!" said Miss Zebra. "It is about people who help to keep us healthy."

"I like helping people!" said Zara Penguin.

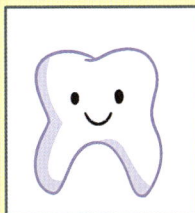

People who
help us

"This is a dentist," said Miss Zebra. "Dentists are people who help keep our teeth healthy."

Everyone was at the dentist's.

"I am Mrs Yak," said the dentist. "Welcome!"

"I like your big chair," said Zara Penguin.

"You can get in it, if you like!" said Mrs Yak.

So Zara did.

"I need your help, please, everyone!" said Mrs Yak. "Nisha Bear needs a check-up. I am worried because I can't find her."

"We can find her for you!" said Zara.

Everyone went to look.

Zara saw a bear. The bear looked worried.

"Are you Nisha?" asked Zara.

"Yes," said the bear.

"Are you worried about your check-up?" asked Zara.

"Yes, I am!" said Nisha. "What if the check-up hurts?"

"The check-up can't hurt you!" said Zara. "Please go back in with us!"

Nisha went back in with
Zara Penguin.

"Welcome, Nisha!" said Mrs Yak.

"Mrs Yak's big chair is great!" said Zara. "Get in it, Nisha!"

So Nisha did.

Nisha saw Mrs Yak's tools.

"This tool helps clean your teeth and keep them healthy, Nisha," said Mrs Yak. "It is very gentle – look!"

Mrs Yak cleaned Nisha's teeth with the gentle tool.

"Your teeth look very healthy, Nisha!" said Mrs Yak. "And check-ups help us keep our teeth clean and healthy."

"What a great check-up!" said Nisha.

"You get a sticker because you did so well, Nisha!" said Mrs Yak. "And everyone gets a sticker, too, because they helped!"

Zara looked at the dentist in Miss Zebra's book.

"Going to the dentist is great!" said Zara. "I want to go for a check-up!"

"Yes!" said everyone. "Mrs Yak was a great dentist. We liked helping her."

They wanted to go back for a check-up, too!

**How much do you remember about the story of _At the Dentist_?
Answer these questions and find out!**

- Who gets to sit in Mrs Yak's chair first?

- Why is Nisha Bear worried at first?

- What is Mrs Yak's gentle tool for?

- What does everyone get as a thank you for helping?